A Footballer Called Flip

Ian Whybrow

illustrated by Tony Ross

Hodder
Children's
Books

a division of Hodder Headline Limited

For the real Allen Rothwell,
a Head who knew all about
inspiring people.

Text copyright © 2000 by Ian Whybrow
Illustrations copyright © 2000 by Tony Ross

First published in Great Britain in 2000
by Hodder Children's Books

9 10

A Catalogue record for this book is available from the British Library.

ISBN 0340 77890 3

Printed and bound in Great Britain by
Bookmarque Ltd, Croydon, Surrey

The paper and board used in this paperback by
Hodder Children's Books are natural recyclable products
made from wood grown in sustainable forests. The
manufacturing processes conform to the environmental
regulations of the country of origin.

Hodder Children's Books
A Division of Hodder Headline Limited
338 Euston Road
London NW1 3BH

Missing Mr Rothwell

A lot of people used to take the mickey out of me. That was before I got famous. Mr Rothwell was the one who got me famous. Well, partly. Mum and Dad helped, too.

Mr Rothwell was the only teacher in the school who didn't call me Shorty.

Or Nipper. Or "How's Little Jack, then?" Some of them called me Tiger but I knew they didn't mean it. They meant, "Aren't you a funny little lad? Aren't you *small*?"

Not everybody liked Mr Rothwell. They said he was strict. But I liked him best of all – even though I wasn't really interested in football. Not then.

People don't call me nicknames now. Only Flip sometimes, but I don't mind that. Usually they call me Jack. Or Jack Lewis. That's my name. Flip is OK, because doing a backflip is how I got my photo in the paper that first time.

My First Backflip

I found out I could do a backflip
when I was four. It wasn't in a gym
or anything. My mum showed me.
She's full of surprises.

I looked out of the
kitchen window
one day and I
couldn't believe it!
My mum turned
over backwards in
the air. I ran out.

5

I said, "*Mu-um!*"

She looked surprised. She said, "What? What is it?"

I said, "That thing you just did! Do it again!"

She said, "What? My backward handspring? Did you like that? Here, I'll show you how to do it. It's easy."

Then Mum, my ordinary normal mum, went 1-2-3-over, just like that. She said, "I'll bet you could do it if you really want to."

It took her all afternoon, because I kept getting it wrong. But she never stopped trying. And all of a sudden I got it. I could do it. My first backflip. 1-2-3-over. Just like that. Oh yes.

It's the thing I'm famous for now. But that first time was ages ago, way before I found out how much Mum knew about football. And she knew *loads*.

Mr Rothwell's Dream

I found out Mr Rothwell was leaving in assembly. Mrs Matthews, the Head, said, "Children, I'm very sorry to have to tell you that Mr Rothwell will be leaving St Saviour's at Christmas. I'm afraid he insists that it is time for him to retire.

8

"I'm sure you're all going to miss him as much as I shall. But we will just have to make his last term as happy and memorable as possible."

After assembly the teachers came down off the stage and I heard Mr Rothwell say to Mrs Matthews, "Of course, you know what would give me a really good send-off?"

Mrs Matthews said, "What's that, Mr Rothwell?"

He said, "It's just a dream, really. Beating Honnington School in the Cup match. For the first time ever."

Mrs Matthews shook her head. "Wouldn't that be something!" she said. "But Honnington's twice the size of St Saviour's. And the boys in their team are enormous. Our problem is that we're so . . ."

"Small," Mr Rothwell said. "Yes, we always say that, don't we? Small school, small boys. As if that matters!"

4

My Dad

I will tell you about
my dad. He's a dentist.
He likes it. He works
on Saturdays, which is
one reason why he
doesn't play in any
teams, like other dads.

"Secondly," he'd say, "I
can't stand changing rooms. They
remind me of waiting rooms. And
thirdly, I'm not a team player."

And I used to say, "What does that mean?" Because say we went to the beach. And say there were people near us having a kick-about. Then my dad used to go, "Come on," and take me to join in. He said that a game on the beach was different, not like normal team games. He meant you didn't have to dress up, and you didn't need to take the game too seriously.

I remember one time, when our side was getting thrashed. Then the ball came in towards Dad, really high and over to his left. He just  lifted his foot. He lifted it, right above his head. He took the ball down just as if he'd caught it with his hand. Then he laid it on the sand in front of him like a baby.

I said to him, "Wow, Dad! I didn't know you could do that!"

He said, "What, bringing the ball down? It's just a trick. There's nothing to it."

Later on, he showed me. "Eye on the ball. Follow it down. Balance yourself. Ease the ball through the air as it drops."

Oh yes!

Puzzle Questions

I wasn't a team player. A bit like
Dad. I liked doing things on my
own better: making models, playing
computer games, that sort of thing.
Puzzles I liked, too, and problems.
Mr Rothwell noticed that.

You could tell if Mr Rothwell was going to ask one of his puzzle questions in class. He had a special way of standing. He used to put his hands behind his back. Then he would put one foot in front of him and look at it. Then he would start rocking, very gently. Most people in our class, you could hear them saying, "Oh no, not one of his puzzle questions." But I liked them.

One day Mr Rothwell said, "Now listen, class. Yesterday evening a little mouse knocked at my door.

So I opened it and said, 'Can I help you?' And the little mouse said, 'I have a problem. I am trying to build two houses, each with four rooms. The rooms have to be all the same size. But every one of the rooms must be different. And one of the houses must be smaller than the other. How can I do it? Can you help me?'

"I said to the mouse, 'Come back tomorrow. I will ask my class. Someone will think of the answer. And the person who can answer that question will probably be a brilliant footballer.' Now, class, is anybody here in the First Eleven?"

And everybody yelled out . . .

Mr Rothwell said, "One at a time. Hands up. Now, why can't you be in the First Eleven if you're from this class? James?"

James said, "We're only nine, sir. You have to be in the top class."

Roger said, "And we're not big enough."

And Mary Luke said, "Specially Nipper!" and pointed at me.

Everybody burst out laughing. Then Mr Rothwell turned his head – *voom* – like that. They all stopped.

"Tell me, Jack," he said. "What is your advice to my mouse friend?"

I said, "Well sir, I just think that if he's a talking mouse, he should go on telly. Then he'll get lots of money. Then he can pay a builder, and the builder can build his houses any way he wants them."

Mr Rothwell said, "Jack, you should speak to Mr Bullock about being picked for the First Eleven. Because I think you have a footballing brain."

I said, "Why, sir?"

He said, "You've got a quick
mind and you have surprising ideas.
You come at things from unexpected
angles. That's what you need to be
a good footballer. Think differently
– surprise the defence, get round
them, open them up. I'm not saying
you don't need good ball control,
because you do. But then – I
happen to know you've got that as
well as a brain, lad."

I said, "How come,
sir?"

He said, "Conkers!"

I said, "Oh, that."

Conkers!

Did I tell you about Mr Rothwell being strict? Well, he was.

There were these conker trees all along the side of our playing fields.

You could pick up the conkers
when they fell down, but you
weren't allowed to
throw sticks at
them. That was all
Ben Walsh's fault
for chucking a
branch up, and
needing five stitches
in his head when it came down.

So anyway, Richard – he was my
friend – was standing under one of
the conker trees pointing up. He
had his football under his arm. He
said, "Look at all the conkers, just
hanging up there. And there's not a
single one on the ground down
here. It's not fair."

I said, "Stand over there, Rich. Now lob the ball to me. Not hard. Keep it low."

So he lobbed it to me. I went – *poom!* – and hit it on the volley. It was one of the tricks Dad showed me on the beach. You keep your eye on the ball as it comes at you at waist-level. You need to shape up well before the ball arrives – get sideways on to your target – then swing your shooting leg nice and smooth. If you want to keep the ball low, you need to get your body over the ball. But I was aiming high, so I leaned back. *Poom!* The ball shot up towards the branch Richard was pointing at.

Suddenly it was raining conkers. Yesssss!

"Run for it!" yelled Richard. We had to, or we would have been buried up to our necks in conkers. Oh yes.

That was when we heard Mr Rothwell shouting. A hundred lines, he gave us. Each. "I should really be giving you two hundred," he said. "But I'll let you off half because you weren't throwing sticks."

Firm but fair, see?

Footballing Brain

Once Mr Rothwell had made his mind up about me being in the First Eleven, he wouldn't stop. Every time I answered one of his puzzle questions, he'd say, "There you are! Footballing brain! When are you going to ask Mr Bullock for a trial?"

One day he was walking along the corridor in front of me with a pile of books.

Suddenly he went, "Timber! Look out!" I ran in front of him and caught the ones that fell off the top. "Nice movement off the ball!" he said. "Have you spoken to Mr Bullock yet?" I think he dropped those books on purpose.

Another time, I noticed our class's pet gerbil, Joey, escape from his open cage. You should have seen him go! If he'd got out of the door, and down the stairs, who knows what would have happened to him? So I jumped over my table and threw myself along the polished floor with my legs sticking out in front.

"Well saved!" said Mr Rothwell, grabbing Joey and popping him back in his cage. "Did you see that, class? A perfect sliding tackle. Right in front of an open goal! Don't you think this boy should be in the First Eleven?"

Everybody went, "Yeah!" But I knew they were just taking the mickey. I knew Mr Bullock would be the same if I went to see him. I hated them all, and I hated football.

Hup Suzie

Dad said not to worry about other people. He said, "Just do your own thing."

Mum said, "I'm not so sure."

We both looked at her.

"Jack's special. He's a natural athlete," she went on. "I mean, think how good he is at Hup Suzie. It's a waste for him not to play in the football team."

Dad said, "I agree he's a natural.

But being brilliant at Hup Suzie doesn't mean he's got to play in a football team if he doesn't want to."

Hup Suzie is a game Dad and I invented. We play it sometimes in the kitchen, until Mum makes us stop. The idea is to make our dog, Suzie, dance. She looks so funny when she's up on her hind legs. She's got ears like helicopter blades.

What we do for Hup Suzie is this. Dad rolls a tennis ball across the kitchen table. I have to get to it before Suzie does.

Then I go
"Hup Suzie!"
and flick it over
her head into
her basket without
it touching the ground.
You have to be good
because that dog is like lightning!

"OK, so Jack can beat the dog to the ball," Dad agreed. "But the fact is, he's like me," said Dad. "He's just not a team player."

"Well, I think that's a shame," Mum said. "I think Jack should take his football seriously. I think he should support the school. And he should remember how much winning means to Mr Rothwell."

Dad's Saturday Morning Off

Like I said, Dad never used to close his surgery on Saturdays. But suddenly, one Saturday in November, he did. He got his partner, Mr Drake, to look after his patients for him.

"I just thought maybe we could go and watch St Saviour's play Greenhill."

I said, "Dad, it's raining. And I've got my model to finish."

Dad said, "Well, your mum thinks we should go and support the school." I turned to see Mum putting her puffa jacket on. "Come on, team," she said. "Time for a team effort."

Mum drove us to Greenhill. It wasn't a cup match or anything, only a league game. Mr Rothwell was the only other person on the touchline, apart from Mr Bullock.

"Hello, Jack," he said. Like he was expecting me.

It was *so* boring! We were rubbish. Nobody stayed in their positions or did any marking. Just charged about, everybody chasing the ball, bashing into each other. At half-time, we were 5-0 down.

Mr Bullock had a go at everybody while they sat on the grass panting.

"Hopeless!" he said. "You're like a lot of big girls dancing about. Oh, sorry, Mrs Lewis, didn't see you there. Nice of you to come and give us a bit of support! And don't we need it!"

Mum smiled. "Oh, they're not that bad, Mr Bullock," she said. "Keith there is quick. If he can stay out wide and put in a few crosses to Ashok, I'm sure he can turn their fullbacks. And Alex and Hussein, you could have their number 10 off-side every time he comes forward. But you need to be a bit quicker running out. And you've got to work together."

By the time the ref called everybody out to start the second half, Mr Bullock had made a few changes.

He agreed with Mum that our two tallest players, Kevin and Daley, should drop back to support the defence and pick up any loose balls in the middle. That would leave Ashok and Dev to do the striking.

Things went pretty well in the second half. Ashok scored his first goal of the season. Kevin put in two because Daley kept drawing Greenhill's defenders out of their positions. Final score 6-3.

Mr Bullock was delighted. "I didn't know you had it in you, lads!" he smiled. "All we need now is to get everybody fitter, and we want some better finishing and who knows . . .?"

Suddenly, there was a horrible
scream. "AGH!"

Ashok had put his
foot down a hole
and turned his
ankle. Mr Rothwell
bent down to
inspect the
swelling. "Nasty,"
he muttered.
Then he looked up
at me and lifted his eyebrows. I
knew that look meant it
was up to me now.

Insults

But Mr Bullock picked Trevor Sharp
for the team and asked me to be
reserve. I said no thanks.

Mum was furious with me when
I told her. "This is your chance to
prove yourself!" she said.

"It's just an insult!" I said. "He
doesn't want me. He's only made
me reserve because Mr Rothwell
keeps on at him. Really he thinks
I'm rubbish. Reserves are rubbish.

And the rest of the team just probably think, 'Oh no, we don't want Shorty!'"

Dad put down his knife and fork. He said, "Is that the real problem? Your height?"

My nose started running like it does when I get upset.

"Well, I was your size when I was your age and I used to get upset. 'Mouse' they called me. But look at me now. I'm pretty tall now, wouldn't you say?"

Mum said, "Is that why you're always saying you're not a team player? You didn't join in because the other kids called you names?"

"I think you're probably right," Dad said quietly. "Oh dear."

Mum said, "Well I get fed up being told girls are big wet softies who aren't supposed to like football. So there we are.

"Useless lot, aren't we?" said Dad. He looked at Mum and she looked at me.

"I don't think we're useless," she said. "We're a team, aren't we? We've got a plan. We've got it together."

I said yep, we had got it together.

"So we should get it together for St Saviour's, right? And give Mr Rothwell a proper send-off," she said. "Now, your first training session at school won't be till next week – so I suggest we all start now. We'll warm up first. Then we'll do some sit-ups, some press-ups, some steps, some stretching, some stamina work . . ."

She was dead serious about getting fit. She was tough. Oh yes.

Training

The following Thursday, after school, I turned up at the gym for training.

"Hello, Tiger," said Kevin. "Ready for a good workout, are you?"

I could see he was looking forward to running rings round me.

What he didn't know was that Dad had been giving me a bit of help with my ball control and tackling. Mum had been teaching me about positioning as well as working on my fitness.

"Heads up!" yelled Daley and hammered a ball at me from across the far side of the gym. I ducked. The ball just missed me and caught Kevin on the shoulder.

"Rough game, eh?" grinned Kevin. "Nearly took your head off!"

Mr Bullock's whistle went. For the first ten minutes we did warm-up exercises – touching all the walls, jogging backwards – that sort of stuff. It was nothing compared to what Mum had been putting me through. I think Kevin was a bit annoyed that I wasn't sweating much. We went on to passing practice, dribbling between cones, all that.

Then Mr Bullock suggested we went outside to the pitch and did "striking the ball from the penalty spot", so off we trotted.

Alex and Daley could really smack in a penalty; Kevin, too. Not many were on target but poor old Nev in goal, they didn't half sting his hands when he stopped them.

"Your go, Jack," called Mr Bullock. "Hurry up, lad, we've got to move on."

I could hear giggles behind me. They were thinking, He'll never even get it to the goal-line.

But I trotted up and stroked the ball with the side of my left foot, just like Dad had shown me.

It went up in a lazy loop and curled into the top right hand corner of the net.

Hup Suzy! A voice called, "Jammy!" and Mr Bullock said, "Not bad, son. Just a bit more welly next time, eh? You were lucky the wind caught it there." He blew his whistle and sorted us out for a six-a-side game.

To be honest, I didn't see much of the ball in the first half. I suggested to Trevor that we swapped positions because I was stronger than him on my left foot. "And keep the passing tighter, eh?" I added.

Trev said, "What do *you* know, *reserve*?" But he didn't wander away so much after that. And by the end of the match, he'd scored three times from my through-balls.

Mr Bullock came trotting over. He scruffed my hair and called over my head. He said, "Well done, lads. Long way to go yet but good fight-back. Specially you, Trevor. Three goals, eh? Didn't know you had it in you!"

And did Trevor say, "Did you notice the way Jack laid them on for me, sir?" Did he heck.

When I'd had my shower and was stuffing my kit into my bag, Mr Bullock did come up to me on the quiet. He told me I was doing very well for a little 'un. A proper little Zola, he said I was, a very nice dribbler. Pity I didn't have a bit more height, my heading wasn't up to much. Still, he said he liked the way I read the game. Finally he added, "Er . . . give us your phone number, will you? I'd like to have a word with your mother."

Mum's Tactics

I said to Mum, "I don't understand why you want to help Mr Bullock. He thinks I'm useless and he'll just steal your ideas and pretend they're his."

"I know, but he's only a young chap," said Mum. "People grow up. And the important thing now is helping St Saviour's beat Honnington and giving Mr Rothwell a treat, isn't it?"

So he did ring and he did steal her ideas. I heard her saying how we'd lost the game against Greenhill because we weren't getting control of the middle of the pitch, and because we hadn't really got anyone up front who could get his head on the ball. And how was Jack getting on in training, by the way?

I didn't like her saying that. I didn't want people to say Mr Bullock only put me in the team because my mum asked him to. So I gave her my "Don't you dare!" look.

After that, she just stuck to giving advice. At the end she said, "By the way, Bernard – that's my husband – has just been typing up a letter for the Parents' Association. It's a call for lots of support next Saturday.

And he's also wondering if any other dads would be interested in getting a Fathers' Team together. Or maybe fathers and teachers, if you'd be interested. What do you think?"

13

The Big Match

On the day of the Cup match, St Saviour's had the biggest crowd of supporters they'd ever seen. The linesmen had to keep yelling at them to keep off the touchline.

Good old Dad, his letter had done the trick. Tons of fathers liked the idea of forming a team and they'd all turned up to shout for the school. There was such a buzz, I didn't mind being reserve. Well, not much, anyway.

Mr Rothwell was there, with Mrs Matthews, looking a bit serious. Our lads got nervous when they saw the size of the Honnington team. They were like giants.